# The CHIZZYWINK and the ALAMAGOOZLUM

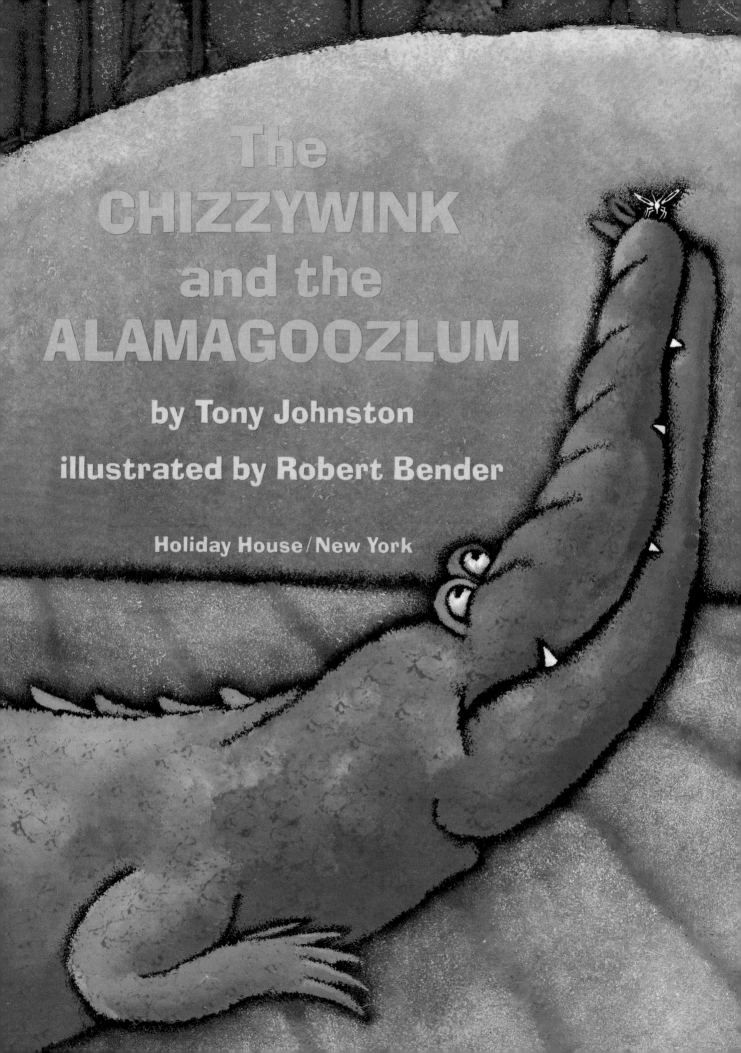

# The CHIZZYWINK and the ALAMAGOOZLUM

by Tony Johnston

illustrated by Robert Bender

Holiday House / New York

Library of Congress Cataloging-in-Publication Data

Johnston, Tony, 1942–

The Chizzywink and the Alamagoozlum / by Tony Johnston;

illustrated by Robert Bender. — 1st ed.

p.     cm.

Summary: A huge mosquito keeps Zeke and Zelda awake, until Zelda

finds a way to quiet the persistent pest.

ISBN 0-8234-1359-4 (hardcover: alk. paper)

[1. Mosquitoes—Fiction.]   I. Bender, Robert, ill.   II. Title.

PZ7.J6478Ch     1998      97-37249      CIP      AC

[E]—dc21

For George and Nora.
And for Rex Mayreis for his expert "librarianship."
T.J.

And special thanks to Martin and Von.
R.B.

Zeke and Zelda lived in an old house deep in the piney woods.

One night they were dozing off when a voice outside called, *"Let me in! Let me in! I want to sip your sweet blood! Yum!"*

When she heard that, Zelda said, "Zounds, Zeke! Fetch the hound! Pile the counterpanes in mounds! I need a mite of sleep!"

So Zeke set the hound beside the door, to keep the varmint out.

He piled another quilt on the bed to mute the sound. Then they
scrooged down under the covers and snoozed again. ZZZZZZ.

But soon the voice called louder still, *"Let me in! Let me in! I want to sip your sweet blood! Yum!"*

Zelda sat up and cried, "Zounds, Zeke! Fetch the hound! Pile the counterpanes in mounds! While you're at it, fetch the tusker! I can't sleep a whisker!"

Zeke set another hound with the first. He fetched their wild boar, too, to keep the whateveritwas out. He piled another quilt on the bed. Then they scrooged way down and snoozed again. ZZZZZZZZZ.

But almost at once the voice boomed, *"Let me in! Let me in! I want to sip your sweet blood! Yum!"*

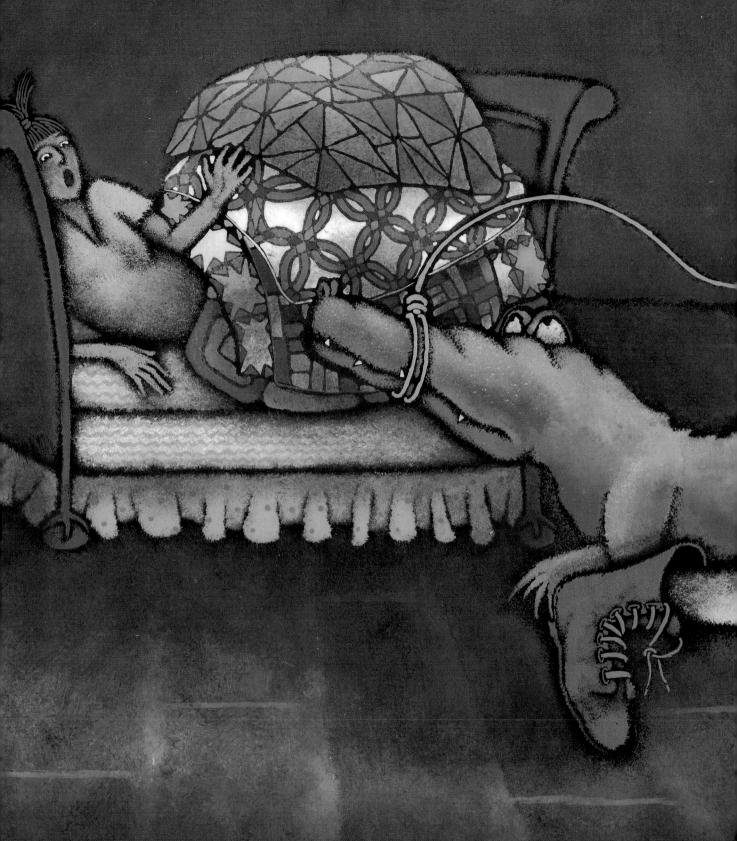

Zelda screeched, "Zounds, Zeke! Fetch the hound! Pile the counterpanes in mounds! Fetch the lizard from the sink! I can't sleep a wink!"

To oblige, Zeke piled more quilts on. He set another hound with the rest. And he hauled the alligator in, to keep the critter out.

They scrooged down to the foot of the bed and soon were snoring again. ZZZZZZZZZZZ.

But that voice droned like a buzz saw through hardwood, *"LET ME IN! LET ME IN! I WANT TO SIP YOUR SWEET BLOOD! YUM!"*

Zelda was grumpy as a woke-up grizzly by then. She hollered,
"ZOUNDS, ZEKE! I CAN'T SLEEP! LET THE BLOODSUCKER IN!"

So he flung the door wide open.

The hounds bayed. The tusker snorted. The alligator bellowed.
For in zoomed — what do you think? An *enormous* chizzywink!

Zeke ducked and screamed, "It's the biggest mosquito I've ever seen!"

It buzzed all over, closer and closer, whining, "Now I'll sip your

But Zelda yelled, "Zounds, Zeke! Do something quick! Fetch the alamagoozlum!"

So he grabbed the jug and poured some.

*"Nothing's sweeter than alamagoozlum! Yum!"*

The chizzywink guzzled till it bloated up, then dozed off on the floor. ZZZZZZZZZZZZZZZ.

As soon as she saw that, Zelda hooted, "Zounds, Zeke! Fetch the broom! Stand back! Give me room!"

She swung with all her might and — swept that chizzywink into the night.

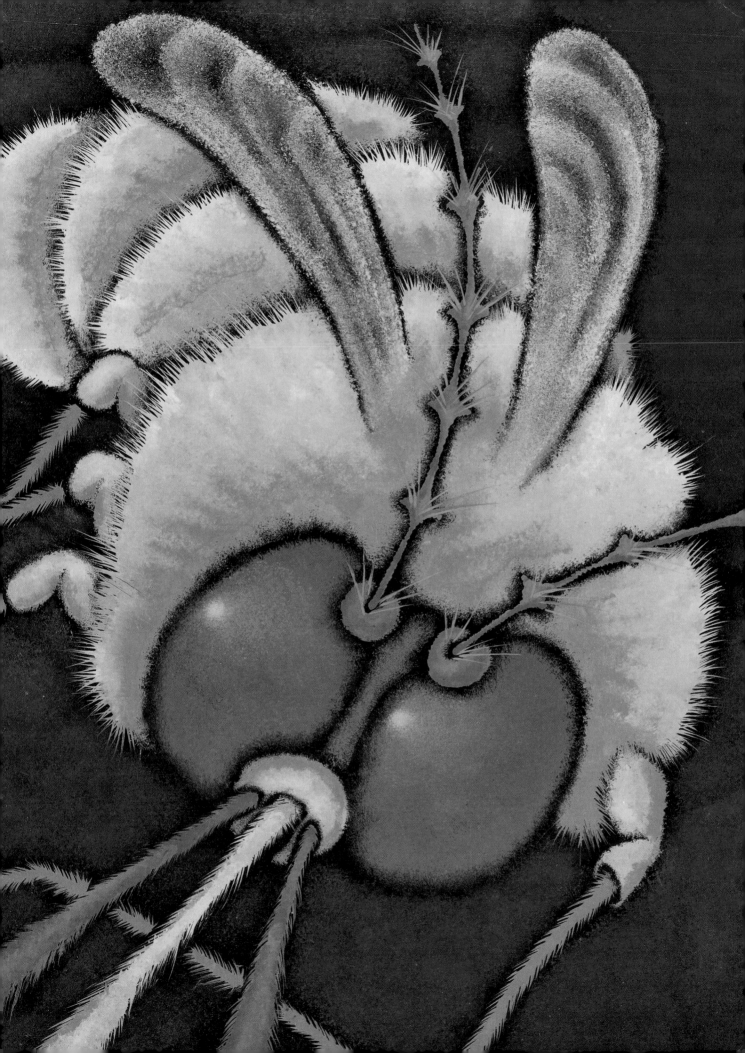

Then they went back to bed.
All was still. Nothing spoke. Nothing buzzed.
But as she closed her eyes, Zelda saw something. She said,
"Zounds, Zeke! I can't sleep! The sun is coming up!"

So they got up, too. They piled flapjacks in a mound, drowned them in syrup, and ate them.

And they both agreed, "Nothing's sweeter than alamagoozlum! Yum!"

A chizzywink is a large mosquito. (Florida)

Alamagoozlum is maple syrup. (Southeastern New York)

W24          A 9/11/00
LC 6/14/17    TC 11

07-98

E      Johnston, Tony
J         The chizzywink and the alamagooz-
       lum.

GAYLORD FG